Benjamin, the Littlest Brother

Dedication

To Lilian, my little sister.

Z. P.

BENJAMIN
THE LITTLEST BROTHER

by Zev Paamoni

*

Illustrated by Alisa J. Yemini

SHULSINGER BROTHERS

NEW YORK

This book was first published in Israel.
The author is an Israeli citizen and was
domiciled in Israel at the time of publication

Printed in Israel 1970.

Set and composed at the Levanda Press Ltd.
Printed by Dfus Offset Israeli Leyetzu Ltd.

ILLUSTRATIONS

Chapter I

Everybody loved Benjamin. Human beings — good or bad, selfish or generous, peaceful or violent — all felt their hearts go out to him when they saw him. Domestic animals crowded up to him and nuzzled him, wild beasts of prey let him pass without harm.

Trees seemed to love him and bent over him protectingly to shade him from the burning sun. The grass seemed to caress him when he rested upon the ground. He could pass through thorn bushes without a scratch. Thistles seemed to draw back their thorns so as not to hurt him.

Benjamin was born near Bethlehem about four thousand years ago. He lived a long and adventurous life. He grew up, married, and had children of his own; but his heart always seemed that of a small child — innocent, trusting and loving.

Bethlehem was located in what was then called the land of Canaan. It is now called Israel. Benjamin was born into a small wandering tribe of sheep herders, who were on their way from north of Jerusalem to Hebron.

Benjamin's father was called Jacob. He was the leader of the tribe. Benjamin's mother was called Rachel. She was a good and beautiful woman, whom the members of the tribe dearly loved. She died in giving birth to Benjamin.

Rachel was deeply mourned by her husband, her family and her tribesmen. She was buried on the spot and a tomb was built over her grave. Rachel's tomb still stands today and is visited by thousands of people who come to Israel every year.

At first, everyone was kind to Benjamin because they were sorry for the poor, little motherless baby. Soon, however, people began to love him for himself, because he was Benjamin and he somehow made them feel good when he smiled at them.

It was Esau, Benjamin's uncle, who first put into words what everyone instinctively felt about the little boy. Esau was Jacob's twin brother and the two were as different as day and night.

Jacob was dark and thoughtful and kind. Esau was red of hair and face, rough and brutal. Esau was a robber chieftan. He and his warlike tribe lived by attacking caravans and robbing them of the goods they carried. Esau and his men would kill the men in the caravans if they resisted or, sometimes, just for fun.

Esau was called Edom — and that name was

spoken of in fear. Many were the terrible tales told around campfires of the dreadful deeds Edom and his men had done.

Benjamin's grandfather, Isaac, had just died in Hebron and Esau had come to attend the funeral. Although Esau had come in peace, everyone was afraid of him. The grownups were afraid of him because they knew who and what he was. The children were afraid of him because he was so big and rough and spoke in a loud and frightening voice.

Esau was sitting with his brother, Jacob, for one final glass of wine together after the funeral, when Benjamin toddled up to him. The little boy looked up at the murderous giant and then smiled at him and patted his face.

Everyone held his breath. Esau was in a bad mood because he had come too late to receive his father's final blessing. When Esau was in a bad mood, no one could tell what he was liable to do. He could snuff out a human life as an ordinary man stepped on a bug.

Esau looked at the little boy, picked him up gently and kissed him. Turning to Jacob, he asked, "This your youngest boy? The one whose mother died?"

"Yes," said Jacob.

"Give him to me," growled Esau. "Come on, you have twelve sons."

"You have more," smiled Jacob.

"That's so," rumbled Esau. "Don't know why I want him. He'll never be a warrior. He's a pipsqueak, just like you were. Go on, you," Esau roared and raised his hand in pretended threat. "Run along, you little flea or I'll crush you."

Everyone expected the little boy to burst into tears of fright. Benjamin stood his ground and kept smiling up at the fearsome giant.

"Look at that," marvelled Esau. "He knows I won't hurt him. I don't know how he knows it, but he knows. Look at him, grinning at me as if I were a baaing lamb."

Esau picked Benjamin up and carried him to his camel. He lifted him high up and put him in the saddle. The little boy laughed loud in delight.

"He isn't afraid of anything," said Esau in amazement. "Sure you won't change your mind and give him to me? No? By all the demons of the desert, I ought to just carry him off. I'd make a man of him. Or..." he added thoughtfully, "maybe he'd make a man of me.

"Here, take the brat." Esau handed Benjamin over to his father carefully. "Take good care of him. He's something special. Goodbye, brother, we'll probably never meet again."

Esau mounted his camel and was off in a cloud of dust. He was right. Esau went off to his domain, the land of Seir, where he ruled the people through violence and fear. Jacob stayed in the land of Canaan and continued living the peaceful life of a sheep herder. The two brothers never met again.

For a long time thereafter, the tribesmen told the tale of the little boy who faced the fearsome Edom and conquered him with a smile.

It was a troubled time, although the troubles passed over the little boy's head because he was too young to understand what was going on. His father, Jacob, had taken over Isaac's tribe and his family had taken its place as the ruling clan of the tribe.

Jacob was having trouble keeping his rebellious sons in order, too. The older ones: Reuben, Simeon, Levi and Judah were continually challenging their father's authority. They fought among themselves, too. It was a troubled time.

With all the tension going on, sometimes little notice was taken of Benjamin's comings and goings. Dina, his older sister, loved him and took care of him; but she had her own troubles, too.

One day, when two mealtimes passed and no

Benjamin showed up, his sister got worried and went looking for him. She could not find him anywhere and went to her father to report the little boy missing. She wouldn't go to her older brothers. She hated them. But that's another story.

Jacob asked the brothers who were guarding the sheep if they had seen Benjamin. Yes, they had, some time ago. They thought he had gone back to the tents to eat.

"He must have wandered off into the hills," said Jacob worriedly. "Reuben and Simeon, go look for him."

Reuben and Simeon trailed Benjamin over one hill and across the next. After about an hour, they saw a sight that made their hearts stop beating. There, across the valley, too far for an accurate bowshot, they saw their little brother.

With a beatific smile on his face, he was toddling amiably toward a crouching mountain lion.

Chapter II

The mountain lion was crouched, tensed, ready to spring. His tail twitched from side to side. His upper lip was lifted in a snarl, showing his cruel curved teeth, teeth that could tear the life from a little boy in one, blood-drenched second. A low growl came from his tawny throat.

Benjamin showed his teeth, too. Little, white, pearly teeth they were; and his wide smile revealed all the teeth he had. He never faltered, but kept on toddling toward the crouching lion.

"Shoot, in God's name," whispered Simeon. "Shoot !"

"It's too far away," Reuben whispered back, "I'm liable to hit the child."

"He's as good as dead, anyway," breathed Simeon frantically. "Shoot, man, quickly."

Reuben unslung his bow and fitted an arrow to the bowstring. He had to do it slowly and quietly so as not to alarm the mountain lion. He hurried as much as he could. The lion would spring any second.

Then the watching brothers saw something that made their eyes pop and their jaws drop. Little Benjamin reached the lion and stood close to him. Slowly, ever so slowly, the mountain lion relaxed his tense muscles and sank back to rest upon his haunches.

Benjamin reached up and patted the lion. The beast lay down and rolled over. The sound he made carried clearly across the valley. The blasted lion was purring like a pet kitten.

Simeon's amazement overcame his caution and he blurted out, "It's unbelievable. The hand of God is upon that child."

The sound of his voice alarmed the lion and he sprang to his feet with a snarl. He glanced across at the brothers and, quick as a flash, he bounded off and was gone.

Reuben and Simeon hurried across to their little brother. Benjamin waited for them with a welcoming smile. He called their names as closely as he could pronounce them, "Oodem, 'Imon."

"You pesky little brat," said Simeon. "Wandering off like that. You could have gotten yourself killed. I ought to spank your bottom."

The tenderness with which he lifted up his little brother and kissed him belied his rough words. Reuben took the little boy from him and placed him upon his shoulders.

"Come on, lion tamer," he said, "I'll give you a ride home."

Benjamin hung on to Reuben's long hair and chanted, "Yo, yo, yo," in imitation of a camel driver's call.

"Look at him," laughed Reuben. "He thinks I'm a camel."

14

"Well," said Simeon judiciously, "You look like a camel and you smell like a camel. How's the poor boy to know you're not a camel."

Since crude taunts and rough insults were part of the accepted daily life among the brothers, Reuben ignored Simeon's rude comment and mused, "I wonder what that lion was doing this far down. They usually don't leave the mountains."

"Probably sneaking down to see if he could carry off a stray lamb," said Simeon.

"Well, Benjamin talked him out of that," Reuben laughed. "Didn't you, you little scamp?" Reuben jogged up and down.

"Yo, yo, yo," said Benjamin.

'Wasn't that something, though," said Simeon, "the way he walked up to that mountain lion. Who'll believe us when we tell them?"

"Do you blame them?" said Reuben. "I didn't believe it myself when I saw it."

"Uncle Esau was right," said Simeon. "That boy is something special."

They came out of the foothills into the valley where the sheep were grazing. The other brothers crowded around them, all asking questions and making sure that Benjamin was unhurt.

Joseph was standing a little apart from the rest of his brothers and Benjamin saw him from his vantage point on Reuben's shoulders. He stretched out his little arms and called, "Sef, Sef."

"Give him to me," said Joseph. "He should be taken to Dina. He's probably hungry. And father should be told that he's been found."

"Who are you to give orders, you strutting peacock?" snarled Simeon. "You're not chief of the tribe — yet."

"And you're not going to be," growled Judah, "if I have anything to say about it."

"Sef, Sef," Benjamin called.

Reuben put him down and he ran over to Joseph and climbed up into his arms. Joseph walked off carrying Benjamin, without replying to his brothers by so much as a look.

"Look at him, the stuck-up popinjay," sneered Levi. "He'll probably tell father he found Benjamin. Maybe father will give him another striped coat, with prettier colors." Levi spat in disgust.

"Stop it, all of you," Reuben said commandingly. "What have you got against him anyway? He does his share of the work."

"Reuben, you're the oldest, but you can't stop me from talking," said Simeon, "and I'll say whatever I please to whomever I please. What have I got against Joseph? Only one thing — he's too blamed smart. Look at how he's gotten around the old man. Father has had that striped coat especially made for Joseph. You know what that means."

"He's picked Joseph for the next leader of the tribe, that's what," said Levi.

"Over my dead body," said Judah.

"Maybe Joseph can arrange that, too," smiled Levi spitefully.

"He isn't man enough to kill me," growled Judah.

"No," said Levi, grinning, "but he's smart enough to get someone to do it for him."

"Another thing," said Simeon. "Those dreams of his, where we're always bowing down to him. When he starts talking about his dreams, I want to push his teeth down his throat."

"Father told him off after the last one, didn't he?" said Reuben. "The one about the sun and the moon and the eleven stars bowing down to him."

"Some telling off," Levi chortled. "A gentle slap on the wrist."

"Well, what did you expect ?" asked Reuben in exasperation. "What do you expect father to do — kill him ?"

"I wouldn't mind if he did," said Judah slowly.

"I wouldn't mind killing him myself," said Simeon matter-of-factly.

"Stop talking nonsense," said Reuben sharply. "Do you want to hear about Benjamin and the mountain lion or don't you?"

Chapter III

Benjamin loved all living things. But, as he grew up, he began to love his brother, Joseph, more than any other human being. Not only because Joseph was clever and told wonderful stories and made up fascinating games, but because Joseph needed someone to love him.

Joseph had ten older brothers. They withdrew from him, so he was lonely. They hated him, so he was miserable. They menaced him, so he was afraid. He was too proud to show his feelings, so he appeared aloof and contemptuous.

He was dissatisfied with his life, not only because his brothers made his life miserable, but because he felt unexplained stirrings in his soul. He felt that he was destined for something greater than a sheepherder's life. He dreamed great dreams and could not tell anyone about them when he awoke because his brothers made fun of them and his father rebuked him.

Joseph turned his dreams into stories and told them to his little brother, Benjamin, telling them as though they were made up stories that had happened to somebody else, long ago and in a far-off land. Benjamin loved the stories and felt the sadness in Joseph.

He knew that his big brother was sad and did not know why. He could only stroke his face and say softly, and proudly — because he could now pronounce his name correctly, "Jo-seph, Jo-seph."

Joseph would hug and kiss his little brother then. Benjamin made him feel that there was one of God's creatures in this cold, unfriendly world that really loved him, just because he loved him, for no particular reason.

His father loved Joseph because he was proud of his son and expected him to lead the tribe some day. His sister, Dina, loved Joseph because she hoped that he would grow up and carry out her vengeance on her older brothers for having killed the man she loved. Benjamin loved Joseph just because he loved him.

Then tragedy struck. The pasturage had given out in the valley of Hebron and Jacob had sent the ten older brothers to graze the flocks farther north. He kept Joseph and, of course, Benjamin, at home with him.

As the weeks and months went by and he heard no word from them, Jacob began to worry. He sent Joseph to look for them and bring back word as to how the brothers and the flocks were doing. Joseph never came back.

The brothers brought back his striped coat of many colors to Jacob and told of having found it in one of the fields. The coat was stained with blood. Reuben, as spokesman for the brothers, said, "An evil, wild beast must have killed him."

Jacob looked around at the circle of his sons' faces. Some assumed a look of exaggerated innocence, some showed no feeling at all, and others were openly triumphant.

"Yes," said Jacob, looking at them. "An evil wild beast killed him."

He went broken-heartedly into his tent and mourned his son. Long after the customary mourning period had passed, he still wore the sackcloth mourning costume. He refused food and drink and stayed in his tent, speaking to no one. Everyone feared that he would die of grief.

Little Benjamin, against strict orders, slipped into his father's tent when no one was looking. He sat down beside his father. Jacob gave no sign. He stroked his father's face with his little hands. Jacob gave no sign.

"Father," said Benjamin quietly, "I loved Joseph, too."

Somehow, that simple statement, made with absolute childish sincerity, caused the stone that had formed around Jacob's heart to melt. He wept. He flung himself face-downward upon his couch and wept and wept.

Benjamin sat on the ground beside him and held his hand. When Jacob had finished weeping, he sat up and said to Benjamin, "Go, my son. Leave me now."

"No, father," said Benjamin, "I won't leave you. I will stay here with you. And I won't eat either. And we will both die together."

Jacob laughed weakly. Then, when he looked at Benjamin, he realized that this was no childish boast. The boy loved him. He knew what he was saying and meant every word he said.

"We can't have that, can we?" said Jacob, getting to his feet. "Come, let's see if we can find something to eat in this sorrow-stricken camp."

From that day onward, Jacob and his youngest son were close. The other sons did not seem to mind. They had resented Jacob favoring Joseph. But Benjamin was just a child. Besides, everyone loved Benjamin.

Jacob suspected that the older brothers had

killed Joseph, but he had no proof and knew he could never get any. Besides, even if he had proof, what would he or could he do about it?

His sons were grown and hard to discipline. If they felt themselves threatened, they would rebel completely. In any case, he was sure his beloved Joseph was dead and nothing that he could do would bring him back to life. If his sons were murderers, then God would take vengeance.

That was, perhaps, the one thing that made this tribe of Jacob's different from the other nomadic tribes that were wandering in and about the land of Canaan about four thousand years go. They believed in one God — and an invisible one, at that.

All the other tribes had many gods; and you could see them. There they stood — statues of stone or wood. Men made sacrifices before their altars and, if the sacrifices were pleasing to the gods, the men's prayers were answered.

Not Jacob's God, though. He was a God of the spirit, not a statue. Jacob had built altars and sacrificed a lamb, a ram, or bullock to this God. Not before a statue of God, but before God himself.

Jacob, in his time of grief, turned more and more to his God for solace — as so many men have done since. Benjamin was close to him and an eager

24

listener to any kind of a story. So Jacob began to tell his youngest son about their special God.

"Many, many, many years ago," Jacob began, "God appeared to your great-grandfather, Abraham."

"I thought you said God couldn't be seen," objected Benjamin.

"He can be seen when He wants to be seen," explained Jacob patiently.

"Have you ever seen Him, father?" asked Benjamin.

"Yes," said Jacob.

"And spoken with Him?"

"Yes." Jacob was sunk in thought for so long that Benjamin had to prompt him.

"Go on about great-grandfather, Abraham."

"Well, God appeared to him, when he was living in a city called Ur, and He said to him: I am the Lord God. I want you to leave your father's house and the land where you were born and go to the land of Canaan."

"And did he go, father?"

"He obeyed God. For the rest of his life, he always obeyed God."

Chapter IV

As often as he could, Benjamin would come to his father's tent after the day's work was done. They would sit in front of the tent and enjoy the cool of the evening. As the stars came out and the sheep settled down for the night, Jacob would talk and Benjamin would listen — and ask questions.

Jacob told Benjamin of Abraham's wanderings, of his trials and troubles, of his battles and his triumphs, and of the covenant the Lord had made with him.

"The Lord promised Abraham that the land of Canaan would belong to his children. When his son, Isaac — your grandfather — was born, Abraham decided to settle down. He founded the city of Beer Sheba, the city of the seven wells."

"I have heard so much about Beer Sheba," Benjamin said eagerly. "When will I see it? When will we go there?"

"Soon," said Jacob. "We'll start moving south very soon. I want to get to Beer Sheba before the rains start."

"Tell me more," said Benjamin.

"It's getting late," said Jacob doubtfully. "You ought to be getting to bed."

"Just a little more," pleaded Benjamin.

It was hard to deny Benjamin anything when he smiled at you. Besides, Jacob loved talking — and his favorite subject was the Lord of heaven and earth, the God of the tribe of Israel.

"Well, after Abraham had dug the seven wells of Beer Sheba and settled down and his son, Isaac, was a little older than you are now; the Lord appeared to Abraham and told him to take his only son, Isaac, whom he loved, and to sacrifice him on an altar on Mount Moriah."

"What did he do ?" asked Benjamin breathlessly, his eyes as round as saucers.

"He obeyed God. He took Isaac to Mount Moriah and prepared to sacrifice him on the altar he built there."

"And Isaac," asked Benjamin. "What did Isaac do?"

"When Abraham explained to Isaac that it was the Lord's will," said Jacob, smilling a little, "Isaac did not resist. He offered his throat to the sacrificial knife."

"And did Abraham kill his son?"

"No. An angel of the Lord stopped his hand at

the last minute. They sacrificed a ram, instead of Isaac."

"Father," said Benjamin thoughtfully, "if the Lord told you to sacrifice me, would you do it?"

Jacob smiled and turned the question aside skillfully. "If I said to you that the Lord had commanded me to sacrifice you, what would you do?"

"I don't know," said Benjamin slowly, "I don't know."

"Would you try to resist? Run away?"

"I don't know. I don't want to die."

"Isaac wanted to live, too. Abraham loved his son and didn't want to kill him."

"Then why did they..."

"Because the Lord must be obeyed. Always, immediately and without question."

"Why, father?"

"God is God and man is man. God knows everything. Man knows nothing."

Benjamin was silent and thoughtful for a long time. Jacob finally said to him, "It's time you went to bed, my son." Benjamin drew a deep breath and stood up.

"Father," he said as he was about to go, "Why did God command Abraham to sacrifice his son?"

"We don't know why God does things. "Or," he

added softly and sadly, "why He permits some things to happen."

"Why do you think He does, father?"

Jacob smiled and said, "I asked my father, Isaac, that same question."

"And what did he say?"

"He said that God is always testing man."

Benjamin remained standing, looking up at the stars. Finally he said slowly, "Father, you said God knows everything."

"He does."

"Then why does He have to test man? Doesn't He know how the test will come out?"

"He does."

"Then why? Why make the test if He knows how it will come out?"

Jacob looked soberly at his youngest son before saying, "I don't know if you're old enough to understand."

"I'll try father."

"When I asked you before what you would do if I said that God commanded me to sacrifice you, you said 'I don't know', didn't you?"

"Because I don't know, father. I don't know what I would do."

"But God knows, son. He knows what you would

do. So if He made the test He would be making it — not for Himself — but for you."

"For me?" asked Benjamin, puzzled.

"Yes," said Jacob earnestly. "For you. He wants you to know what you would do. You won't know unless He tests you."

"It seems like a hard way."

"It is a hard way. Because life is hard. And learning is hard. And only in struggling to pass His test do we learn about ourselves. About what we can do. We must know that we can do one thing before we can go on to the next — the harder — one."

"I don't understand that, father."

"It's late and you're tired. Or it's early and you're young. In any case, good night, son."

"Good night, father," Benjamin turned to leave and then turned back.

"Did God test you, father?"

"Yes."

"Will you tell me about it?"

"I will. Sometime. Now, go to bed."

"Father, when I asked you before what you would do if God commanded you to sacrifice me, you didn't answer."

"I didn't have to. I think you know."

"Good night, father."

"Good night, son."

As Benjamin walked through the camp, he passed Dina's tent. From within he heard a muffled sobbing.

"Dina," he called softly, "Is anything the matter?"

"No," Dina's tear-choked voice answered. "Nothing. Go away."

"I won't go away, Dina," said Benjamin, "I'm coming in." He went into his sister's tent.

Chapter V

It was dark in Dina's tent. Benjamin could barely make out Dina's form, lying on her couch with her head pillowed on her arms. She was crying uncontrollably and trying to muffle her sobs by crying into a cushion.

"Why are you crying, Dina?" Benjamin asked.

Dina did not answer immediately. When she finally was able to speak, she said bitterly, "Because I wish I were dead."

Benjamin made no reply. He just stood there waiting. Dina sat up and said, a little more calmly,

"Benjamin, go away and leave me alone. It must be very late and you ought to be in bed."

"No, Dina," said Benjamin, "I won't go. You're sad and when people are sad they shouldn't be alone."

Dina held out her arms to him. He came to her and she kissed him tenderly and rocked him in her arms as she had ever since she had taken over the care of the motherless little Benjamin. She smiled in spite of herself.

"Benjamin," she said, with a laugh that was half a sob, "you're such a little boy. Where did you learn your wisdom ?"

"What wisdom?" asked Benjamin. "I love you, dear sister, and when you are sad, my heart hurts."

"Little darling," said Dina, kissing him again. "You're the only decent human being in this camp of murderous wild beasts."

"You're wrong, Dina," said Benjamin earnestly. "People are good — when they forget to be bad."

Dina laughed outright. It was a laugh of amusement and not of bitterness. She stroked her little brother's head.

"You're beginning to talk nonsense," Dina said. "You must be sleepy. Go to bed."

"I'm tired and I'm sleepy," said Benjamin, "but I won't leave you as long as you're sad."

"I'm not sad any more," said Dina. "You've cheered me up. Now run along, little brother. Good night."

"Why were you crying, Dina?" Benjamin asked.

"You're too young to understand," said Dina shortly.

"I don't have to understand," said Benjamin, "Tell me anyway. You hardly ever talk to anyone."

"There's no one to talk to," said Dina bitterly, "No one but you — and you're such a little boy yet."

"Talk to me anyhow," said Benjamin. "Tell me why you were crying."

Dina was silent for a long time. It was very quiet. There was no noise from outside. All the men and animals were asleep. Benjamin had almost nodded off when Dina spoke.

"I was crying," she said quietly, "because Joseph is dead."

"Even father has stopped mourning him," said Benjamin.

"I shall never stop mourning him," Dina said intensely. She was speaking to herself now and not to Benjamin. "Joseph was my last hope. If he had lived, he would have had to kill Simeon and Levi.

But they killed him first, the murdering swine !"

"Why do you want Simeon and Levi killed?"

"Because they killed the man I loved," Dina burst out sobbing afresh, "the only man I ever shall love."

"Why did they kill him ?" asked Benjamin.

"Because they're murderers," her eyes flashed hatred in the dark. "They like killing. They're not like our father at all. They're more like Uncle Esau."

"Tell me about the man you loved," said Benjamin.

The hatred seemed to leave Dina's eyes. Her face became soft with memory. Once again, Benjamin was almost asleep before Dina started to speak.

"He was handsome — and tall. The first time I saw him, I thought to myself: This is how the angel father told us about must have looked. It all happened long ago before you were born.

"His name was Shechem. He was a prince of the Hivite tribe. I knew it was wrong to marry him without father's consent. But I loved him so much I couldn't help myself.

"I knew I was doing wrong by marrying a man who belonged to tribe of idol worshippers. But Shechem was so good and kind. He was the finest man I ever knew. And he was killed because of me."

Once more, sobs tore Dina's throat. She let go of Benjamin, threw herself down upon her couch and wept heartbrokenly. Benjamin stroked her hair.

"Dear Dina," he said softly, "don't cry any more. Please don't cry any more."

After a while, Dina stopped crying. She sat up and dried her eyes. Benjamin said, "Go on, Dina. Tell me what happened."

"Shechem's father, the leader of the Hivite tribe, welcomed me as a daughter," Dina continued. "He said that he would go to see father and arrange everything peaceably. He did just that. They agreed that the Hivite tribe would put away their idols and follow our God. Then the two tribes could become one and our marriage would be celebrated. Father agreed."

"Then what happened?" asked Benjamin.

"Simeon and Levi would not agree. They said the marriage was a dishonor to the tribe. They led a raiding party into the city and killed anyone who got in their way. They slaughtered Shechem and his father before they could draw their swords and dragged me back and shamed me before the entire tribe."

"What did father do?" asked Benjamin.

"What could he do?" answered Dina bitterly, "All of my brothers were united against him. Besides, it was too late. He had to think of the tribe. We had to move before the surrounding tribes gathered to take revenge upon us for the killing."

"Did the other tribes make war on us?"

"No, they didn't dare. They were afraid of Uncle Esau, I suppose. We went up to Beth El and on the way back to Hebron, you were born and your mother died. I've tried to be a mother to you ever since."

"You should have married again, Dina," said Benjamin.

"Silly little boy," said Dina, affectionately tousling his hair. "Who'd have me? Besides, I still love Shechem. That is my sin."

"It's no sin to love," said Benjamin soberly.

"Why, listen to the wise old man," said Dina, affectionately mocking him. "And what other pearls of wisdom do you have to give me this late in the night?"

"I'm too tired and sleepy to think of anything right now," said Benjamin. "I'm going to bed. In the morning I'll try to think of something."

"Good night, little brother," said Dina, "and thank you."

"For what?" asked Benjamin in surprise.

"For being the dearest, sweetest little boy in the whole world," said Dina with a smile. Benjamin smiled back.

"Good night, dear sister," he said, and stumbled sleepily off to his tent.

Chapter VI

It was some time after that. Benjamin could not have said how long. People didn't live by the clock and the calendar four thousand years ago. When the sun rose, it was time to get up. When it got dark, it was time to go to sleep. When you were hungry, it was time to eat.

There was a time to plant and a time to harvest. There was a time of rain and cold. There was a time of heat and burning sun. The sun was the clock and the seasons were the calendar. Some Bedouin tribes still live that way in the desert. They don't have clocks and couldn't tell the time if they had them.

Benjamin didn't know how long it was since that night when Dina had told him her story. He hadn't forgotten it, but it had sunk to the back of his mind. There was so much to do, so much going on.

The tribe was on the move again, moving slowly southward toward Beer Sheba, the city of the seven wells, that Abraham had founded. The city that still lives and flourishes while so many other fabled cities of legend have crumbled to dust and disappeared from the face of the earth.

It was evening. The tents had been put up and the flocks were resting nearby, guarded by tribesmen who were on duty that night. Benjamin was sitting in front of his father's tent. He was firing more questions in a minute than his father could answer in an hour. Little boys are like that.

"When will we reach Beer Sheba, father?" Benjamin rattled on. "Is it far?" Is anybody there now? Maybe another tribe has taken over the wells? Will we try to get them back? Do you remember Beer Sheba? How long is it since you were there?"

Jacob did what most fathers do. He answered the last question and let the others go.

"I haven't seen Beer Sheba for a long, long time. The last time I was there I was a young man. And I had to run away in the middle of the night," Jacob smiled a little at the memory.

"Why did you have to run away, father?"

"Because my twin brother, Esau, wanted to kill me."

"Why did he want to kill you?" Benjamin asked breathlessly.

"That's a long story," said Jacob.

"I like long stories," said Benjamin.

"I know you do," smiled his father. "But it's pretty late and my throat is dry."

"It isn't very late," said Benjamin, "and I'll bring you some water." He ran and brought his father a dipperful of water from the well in the center of the camp.

Jacob drank deeply and said gratefully. "Thank you, son. That was just what I needed."

"Now, the story, father," said Benjamin.

"What story?" asked his father teasingly.

"The story about how Esau wanted to kill you. You promised to tell it to me."

"I don't remember promising to tell you any story," smiled Jacob.

"Please, father!"

Jacob sat silently in thought for a while and then he said soberly, "It's not a story that I'm particularly proud to tell. Still, I don't see how I could have done anything else.

"You know that Esau and I were twins. He was the older and, by right, he should have been the leader of the tribe. My father seemed to favor him and that made my mother furious.

"You never knew your grandmother. I'm sorry for that. Her name was Rebecca and she was a wonderful and remarkable woman. She would have loved you very much and I'm sure you would have loved her."

"I know I would have, father," said Benjamin.

"Yes, well. My mother was bound and determined that I, and not Esau, would be my father's heir and lead the tribe. She swore an oath by her life that she would see to it that I should inherit the leadership of the tribe. You know what that means?"

"Yes, father. That means that if what she swore to didn't come true, she would die."

"Exactly. I loved my mother very much and I wanted her to live. So when she insisted that I try to trick my father into giving me the leadership, I agreed — against my better judgement."

"How did you try to trick your father?" asked Benjamin.

"My father was old, and feeble, and almost blind. My mother wrapped goatskins around my neck and arms, so that when my father touched me he would think that he was touching Esau, who — as you saw — is very hairy. She dressed me in one of Esau's hunting costumes and sent me in to receive my father's blessing and to receive the leadership of the tribe from his hands."

"And did you fool your father?"

"Not for a minute," smiled Jacob, "but he pretended to be fooled. He told me to come closer and I did — with my heart in my mouth. Then he ran his hand over me and said: The voice is the voice of Jacob, but the hands are the hands of Esau."

"What did he mean?" asked Benjamin puzzled.

"I didn't understand at the time, either. It took me many years before I could understand. Anyhow, my father told me to kneel down and receive his blessing and the leadership of the tribe. I couldn't believe the trick was succeeding.

"After he had blessed me and recited the formula of transfer of the leadership in the name of our God, he took my face in his hands and smiled at me. Then he said: I would have preferred you to have won the leadership of the tribe in your own name, my son. But this way is as good as any other."

"What happened then, father?"

"I was so ashamed of having fooled my father and having him know it all the time that I went away and stayed by myself for a while. I had to think. I realized that my father had preferred me to Esau all the time, but he knew that if he showed it, Esau would have killed me.

"My father was much wiser than I am." Jacob's voice trailed off as regret and sorrow for his lost son, Joseph, saddened his heart. He came out of his reverie as he realized that Benjamin had repeated his next question three times.

"Did Esau try to kill you, father?"

"He looked all over for me but couldn't find me. My mother came to where I was and told me to run away. I wanted to fight Esau for the leadership of the tribe."

"Fight Esau?" Benjamin asked in astonishment.

"Yes. I was young and strong — and foolish. He probably would have killed me. But my father commanded me to go away to visit my uncle, Lavan, until Esau cooled off and I obeyed my father. Sons obeyed their fathers when I was a boy. Not like this disobedient generation."

"That was a terrible thing, father," said Benjamin, "To have to leave the tribe and go away to a strange land."

"Yes," said Jacob, "But it had its good side. During the journey, our God appeared to me for the first time."

Chapter VII

Jacob was silent for so long that Benjamin could not help saying, "Go on, father. Please."

Jacob seemed to rouse himself from somewhere deep in his memory. He looked at Benjamin as though he were surprised to find him there and said, "It's very late, my son."

"I don't care how late it is, father," said Benjamin intensely. "You can't stop now, father, not in the middle of the story. Please, please go on."

Jacob smiled at his son, at his young, pleading face, at his deep, earnest eyes, at his black, curly hair. Lord God, he looked so much like his mother, Rachel. Dear Rachel, of beloved memory. Jacob sighed deeply and then smiled again.

"No, son," he said, "I shouldn't stop the story, now, should I ?"

"Tell me about how our God appeared to you, father !"

"Well, I was on my way to the land of Haran, where my uncle Lavan lived. I didn't know the road, but I knew I had to keep bearing northeast.

The sun had already set when I came to a place that was then called Luz.

"I was far from any place of human habitation and, rather than risk walking through unfamiliar country at night, I decided to take the lesser risk of spending the night sleeping in the open.

"I took a stone for a pillow, wrapped myself in my cloak against the cold, and settled down to sleep as best as I could. I'm not too sure what happened after that."

"What do you mean, father?" asked Benjamin.

"I mean that I don't know whether I really fell asleep and dreamed or whether I saw a vision with my eyes closed. But suddenly the sky was filled with beautiful light — gold and red and blue light. And there before me was a tall, tall ladder stretching from earth to heaven.

"Beautiful winged creatures were going up and down the ladder. I knew they must be angels of God. My father had seen one once and had described it to me. Now I was seeing dozens, perhaps as many as a hundred.

"I looked along the whole length of the ladder and there — at the very top — stood God."

"How did He look, father?" asked Benjamin breathlessly.

"Who can describe God?" said Jacob. "You see

God, not with your eyes, but with your heart. Some day, my son, I hope you will prove yourself worthy of having God appear to you. Then you will understand what I mean."

"Did God speak to you, father?" Benjamin asked.

"Yes. He spoke to me and His voice echoed in my soul. He said to me: I am the God of Abraham and Isaac. I am your God, now. I shall give this land to your children. Your people will be a great nation. Because of them all the nations of the world will be blessed.

"Then the vision was gone and I was awake and alone in the dark and afraid."

"What did you do then, father?"

"In the morning, as soon as it was light, I got up and built an altar to the Lord. And at the top I put the stone I had used for a pillow. The only thing I had to sacrifice to the Lord was a little jar of oil.

"I poured the oil upon the altar and called the place Beth-El, the House of God. It's been called by that name ever since."

"Did you ever go back there, father?" Benjamin asked.

"Yes," said Jacob. "Just before you were born. The altar was still standing and we sacrificed to the Lord."

"Did you ever see God again, father?"

"Yes. He appeared to me again a number of times after that."

"What did He say to you, father?"

"Many things He told me, my son," smiled Jacob, "but one thing He did not tell me was that I would have a young son called Benjamin, who would torture me with questions all night and would refuse to let me sleep."

Benjamin stood up immediately. He said, "Forgive me, father. It was wrong of me to pester you with questions when you are so tired and want to sleep. I'll leave you now."

Jacob threw back his head and laughed. He held out his arms to his son and, when Benjamin came to him, he held his son and kissed him tenderly.

"Benjamin, little son," said Jacob with a smile, although the tears were not very far from his eyes, "Benjamin, you're all I have left. You're the only one in the world who loves me."

"No, father, you're wrong" said Benjamin earnestly. "Forgive me for contradicting you, but all of my brothers love you. Dina loves you. The whole tribe loves you and respects you and values you."

"Well," said Jacob grimly. "If your brothers love me, they have a peculiar way of showing it.

And Dina? I hardly ever see Dina; and when I do, she doesn't look at me and barely speaks to me."

"Father," said Benjamin seriously. "Don't you think Dina should get married?"

Once again, Jacob threw back his head and laughed loud and long. When he finally stopped, he gasped, between chuckles, "Benjamin, you amaze me. One minute you talk like a little boy and the next minute you talk like an old grandfather."

"Dina is unhappy, father. I've seen her crying."

"Have you, now," said Jacob. "Well, so have I. Perhaps you're right. I'll think about it."

"Thank you, father," said Benjamin.

"It isn't that simple," Jacob said. "There's a lot to it that you don't know about. But I'll see what I can do. Now, suppose you run off to bed and let me handle the affairs of the tribe for a while."

"Good night, father," said Benjamin. "Thank you for telling me about God."

"I like talking to you, son," smiled Jacob. "Good night."

Benjamin went off. He was tired, but he knew he wouldn't sleep. His head was too full of visions of God and His angels going from heaven to earth and from earth to heaven along Jacob's ladder. He decided to take a little walk about the camp to tire himself enough for sleep.

As he walked in the direction of the sheep, he saw his oldest brother, Reuben, in the moonlight. Reuben was slowly beating his fist against an outcropping of rock. Tears were streaming down his cheeks silently.

Benjamin came up silently behind Reuben and said, "What's the matter, Reuben?"

Reuben whirled about, startled, and snarled, "Get away from me, you mangy little cur. Go on, get out of here or I'll knock you head off!"

"You won't hit me, Reuben," said Benjamin quietly. "You won't hit me because I love you."

Reuben sat down and buried his face in his hands. Benjamin came up to him and put his arms about his neck and kissed his big brother.

"Tell me what's the matter, Reuben," Benjamin said.

Reuben raised his head and looked at Benjamin. Speaking as though to himself, he said, "Why not? I've got to talk to someone or I'll go crazy. But by all the demons of the desert, if you ever tell anyone what I'm going to tell you now, I'll strangle you. Do you hear, little Benjamin? I'll strangle you!"

Chapter VIII

Benjamin looked at his brother. Reuben's face was a mask of pain in the bright moonlight. Lines of suffering were black upon his face as though etched indelibly upon it.

"Poor Reuben," thought Benjamin. "Poor, dear brother. His heart is hurting him very badly."

Aloud, he said, "Come, Reuben, get up. Let's go for a walk."

Like a sleepwalker, Reuben rose to his feet and, with his little brother's hand in his, began walking. They passed the guards on the perimeter of the camp with a casual word of greeting. No one would have thought of stopping them. They were the tribal leader's sons.

They walked on. Ordinarily, it was dangerous to walk this far away from the camp into the desert at night. Prowling beasts of prey and desert robbers were a constant danger. Benjamin felt safe with Reuben by his side, though.

Reuben was unusually strong and very brave. Even unarmed, he was equal to overcoming any danger that might arise to confront them. They walked on and on until little Benjamin felt ready to drop in his tracks. He uttered no word of complaint, but he was very glad when Reuben threw himself down upon the cold sand of the nighttime desert.

Grateful for the rest, Benjamin sat down beside him. He sat in silence beside Reuben, waiting for him to start talking. He waited a long time. Finally, Reuben said, "Benjamin, do you remember Joseph ?"

"Yes," said Benjamin, "I remember him."

"You were such a little boy," said Reuben. "I thought you might have forgotten."

"No," said Benjamin, "I haven't forgotten Joseph."

"It was all my fault," Reuben burst forth in an agonized voice, "I am the oldest. I was in charge. I could have stopped it if I hadn't been such a fool !"

"What happened to Joseph, Reuben?"

Reuben looked at Benjamin sharply and said, "Swear you won't tell anyone what I'm going to tell you."

"I swear," said Benjamin evenly, "I swear by the God of my father that I shall never betray you."

Pain was in Reuben's eyes. He shook his head as though to brush away a bitter memory. Desperately, he said, "Actually, it was father's fault in the first place. He should have known better than to send Joseph after us."

"Go on," said Benjamin.

"He came strutting up to us, the blasted popinjay in his pretty striped coat. We saw him coming toward us from far off. We were grazing the flocks near Dothan. Judah and Simeon and Levi wanted to kill him right off."

Horror choked Benjamin. Despite the dryness of his throat, he managed to ask, "Did they kill him?"

"No," said Reuben, "I was the oldest. I was in charge. But I knew it would be stupid to forbid them. They all wanted to kill Joseph. I couldn't have fought them all."

"What happened, Reuben?"

"Well, he came walking up as pretty as you please and said 'Shalom' as though butter wouldn't melt in his mouth. They knocked him down, stripped off his fine coat, and slapped him around a bit.

"Then I stepped in. I said that we shouldn't be guilty of having our brother's blood upon our hands. I frightened them a little with talk about blood guilt. Then I said we could throw him into a pit, there were a lot of them around, and he would die by himself in the wilderness and his blood would not be upon our hands."

"They agreed?" asked Benjamin breathlessly.

"Yes, they agreed. We threw him into a pit and then sat down not far off and ate our lunch. I then went off with my flock, thinking to come back later, pull Joseph out of the pit and send him back to father with a kick in the tail to speed him on his way.

"But the blamed sheep got into trouble in a wadi, the devil gets into their stupid heads sometimes, and by the time I got them all out and rounded up, it was very late. When I got back to the pit, I found it empty."

"Go on, Reuben, go on!"

"I was very angry. I was ready to kill whoever had killed Joseph. But all my brothers swore that they had not killed him. They said that, while I was gone, a caravan came past bound for Egypt. They pulled Joseph up out of the pit and sold him to some Midianite merchants as a slave. The caravan was miles away by now. There was nothing to be done."

"So you came back and showed father Joseph's coat," said Benjamin.

"Yes," said Reuben. "That was goat's blood on the coat. I said we found the coat and that a wild beast had killed Joseph, probably. We all thought

father would die of grief. We were all pretty scared and sorry."

"And that's where Joseph is now," said Benjamin, "a slave in Egypt."

"If he's still alive," said Reuben. "Slaves don't live long in Egypt, I hear. They work them very hard. Slaves are cheap. When one dies, they buy another. Egyptians are rich."

"Poor Joseph," said Benjamin.

"I don't care about Joseph," Reuben said. "We all hated him because of his high and mighty airs and because father made it pretty plain that Joseph was his choice for the next leader of the tribe."

"Poor Reuben," said Benjamin.

"I'm the oldest," said Reuben heatedly. "I'm going to be the next leader of the tribe." He stood up and glared about him as though looking for someone who would challenge his leadership.

Benjamin said nothing. Reuben sat down slowly with his head in his hands. Slowly he said. "What kind of a leader will I be? I can't even control my younger brothers. How will I be able to control a whole tribe? I'm afraid I'll lead the tribe to disaster."

"No, you won't, Reuben," said Benjamin. "There's no one stronger or braver than you in the tribe. You will lead the tribe and our God will lead you."

Reuben had to smile in spite of himself. Tousling his little brother's hair affectionately, he said, "What do you know of our God, snippet?"

"Father's been telling me about Him," said Benjamin.

"I saw father sacrificing to God at the altar in Beth-El before you were born," said Reuben soberly. "He's a very holy man, our father."

"Yes," said Benjamin. "God appeared to him and spoke to him."

"God would never speak to me," said Reuben abjectly. "My brother's blood stains my hands." Reuben looked at his hands and then clenched them tightly.

Benjamin put his little hand upon his brother's big fist. He said thoughtfully, "I think that if someone loves God enough, God is bound to love him too."

Chapter IX

Reuben regarded Benjamin in puzzlement. He still thought of his little brother as a baby and to have him talking like a grownup was a little unsettling. He asked, "Who told you that? Father?"

"No," said Benjamin. "No one told me. But that's how it is with people and animals. If you love them, they love you. It must be the same way with God."

"Funny little Benjamin," Reuten smiled. "Do you remember how you walked up to that mountain lion and made him purr like a pet kitty?"

"I've heard the story so often," said Benjamin. "It seems to me as if I remember."

"Mountain lions live by killing and eating sheep. Do you think that sheep ought to love mountain lions?" asked Reuben teasingly, then his voice grew more heated, "Do you think a man should love those who hate him and want to harm him? Kill him?"

"If you love someone," said Benjamin stubbornly, "he won't hate you and he won't want to harm you."

"Then you think that a hungry mountain lion won't kill a lamb if the lamb loves him?" asked Reuben with a chuckle.

"I don't know," said Benjamin. "Maybe I'll know when I'm older."

"Well, you won't grow up unless you get some sleep," said Reuben. "Come on, little camel driver, up on my back and I'll give you a ride home."

Reuben swung Benjamin up onto his shoulders. Benjamin put his arms about his big brother's neck and chanted sleepily, "Yo, yo, yo," as Reuben started walking with long, vigorous strides back to the camp.

"I feel much better," said Reuben in surprise, "much better. Just talking about it helped, I guess. Now remember, Benjamin, if you ever repeat a word of this to anyone..."

Benjamin snored softly. Reuben put up a hand to hold him steady so that he would not fall off his shoulders in his sleep and walked rapidly back to camp.

When he reached the encampment, the guards recognized him and greeted him respectfully. Reuben returned their greeting cheerfully and strode on with the sleeping Benjamin on his shoulders.

"Feeling a lot better coming back than he did going out," said one of the guards to his companion.

"It's that little Benjamin," said the other guard. "Sometimes it cheers me up just watching him and listening to him laugh. Wish I had a son like him. Come on, it's time for another turn around the camp. Quiet tonight, but you never know." The two moved off, looking watchfully out into the desert.

Reuben strode through the camp. He was holding Benjamin in his arms. The little boy was fast asleep. Dina was standing in front of her tent as Reuben passed it. Hatred blazed in her eyes at the sight of him.

"Give him to me," she said imperiously. "I'll put him to bed."

For some reason that he could not explain, Reuben felt guilty as he looked into her eyes. He felt that he had to make some sort of explanation. He said hesitantly, "We were talking and he fell asleep. I just..."

"I don't care to talk to you, any of you," Dina said with compressed lips. "Just give him to me and go away."

Benjamin stirred in Reuben's arms and murmered sleepily, "Dina — Reuben, love each other. Please love each other." He snuggled closer to Reuben and fell asleep again.

"You still hate us," said Reuben wonderingly. "After all this time, you still hate us."

"Yes," Dina hissed. "And I'll never stop until I see you lying dead before me just as he lay dead before me."

"Dina... sister," Reuben said helplessly.

"Sister wasn't the name you called me when you dragged me back and shamed me before the tribe," said Dina fiercely. "Now just give me the boy and go."

Reuben handed Benjamin over to her. She staggered a little beneath his weight and shifted her hold. Benjamin was getting too big to carry. She hadn't realized how much he had grown.

"Good night, sister," said Reuben.

Dina hesitated for a moment in the entrance of her tent and then went in without answering him. She put little Benjamin down upon the couch, took off his sandals and covered him with a sheepskin against the cold of the night.

As she kissed him good night, Benjamin opened his eyes and said softly, "Dina, you hate too much and don't love enough. You should get married."

"All right, you little match maker," Dina laughed at him fondly. "You find me a man who's as good and kind as you are and I'll marry him in a minute."

"I'll try," promised Benjamin, as he drifted off to sleep.

"It won't be easy, little brother," whispered Dina. "There's no one like you in the whole world." She gave the sheepskin a final tug to adjust it just so and went off to her own bed.

In the morning, as Dina was crouched over the

fire making breakfast, Benjamin came to her leading a rather ragged and dirty little boy.

"Please make a big breakfast, Dina," Benjamin said. "This is my friend, Uzi. I've invited him to have breakfast with us."

"Very well," said Dina, "as long as his mother knows where he is."

"He doesn't have a mother," said Benjamin.

"Oh?" said Dina.

"My mother is dead," said Uzi importantly.

"I see," said Dina.

"She has been dead almost a year," Uzi said, "When she has been dead a whole year, my father will make a special sacrifice in her memory. He told me so."

"You probably haven't washed since your mother died," said Dina. "Can you wash yourself?"

"Of course I can," said Uzi. "When I remember."

"Well, you try and put your mind to it before breakfast," said Dina.

She busied herself with preparations for breakfast. When it was ready, she called to the boys to come and get it. Only Benjamin appeared.

"Where is your friend?" Dina asked.

"I don't know," said Benjamin. "Maybe he went to wash."

"He could have had ten baths by this time," said Dina. "Breakfast's ready and we won't wait."

Just then, Uzi came along. He hadn't washed. He was leading two boys, smaller and dirtier than he was, and he was carrying a little girl.

"These are my two brothers and my sister," Uzi explained. "They're hungry, too."

Chapter X

Dina didn't know whether to laugh or cry. She did neither. She compressed her lips sternly and said, "Nobody gets a bite to eat until they're clean."

"Dina," said Benjamin gently, "being dirty doesn't hurt as much as being hungry."

"Oh, all right, all right," said Dina brusquely, not wanting to show that she was ashamed of helself. "Sit down, all of you, I think we have enough to go around if nobody asks for seconds."

For the next quarter of an hour or so, there was silence — except for the sounds made by hungry children eating. Dina looked into the pot and announced, "There are seconds after all for anyone who wants some."

Four bowls were held up immediately. Dina

portioned out what was left, explaining, "Seconds are never as large as firsts."

After breakfast, Benjamin and Uzi were sent to the well for water and breakfast dishes and children were well scrubbed. Clothes were washed and hair was combed. The sun was quite hot by now and the clothes dried quickly.

Dina surveyed the results of her handiwork and thought, "Why, they're nice looking children. The boys are quite good-looking. Unfortunately, the little girl is — well, if one must come right out with it — the little girl is downright homely. It doesn't seem fair. It doesn't matter if boys aren't handsome. But little girls should all be born pretty. She has a charming smile, though."

She was sitting in the shade, holding the little girl in her lap while the boys played a game that entailed quite a bit of running and shouting, when their father came along.

Dina knew him slightly. He was a distant relation — almost all of the members of the tribe were related — by the name of Arieh. He was a warrior of the tribe and quite well regarded. Dina remembered now. His wife had died giving birth to the little girl and he had been having a rather hard time of it ever since.

"Your pardon, Miss Dina," Arieh addressed her

respectfully, as was due to the chieftan's daughter, "I've just come off night guard duty and I've been looking for the kids everywhere. I'm sorry they bothered you."

"They didn't bother me at all," smiled Dina. "They're very well-behaved children."

"That's news to me, ma'am," Arieh grinned back at her. "I'll take them off your hands now."

"Why don't you leave them here," said Dina. "You need to sleep after being up all night. And the best-behaved children make some noise."

"That's very kind of you, Miss Dina," said Arieh, "But I couldn't..."

"Have you had breakfast yet?" Dina interrupted him.

"Well, no, ma'am," said Arieh. "You see, I've been looking all over for the kids and I didn't get a chance..."

"Have some with us," said Dina curtly. "I think we're about ready for a second breakfast, aren't we, children?" There was a chorus of enthusiastic agreement from the children.

"Hold your daughter," said Dina, handing him the little girl. "It will be ready in no time. Benjamin and Uzi, down to the well for more water."

"This time," said Uzi, as he left with a bucket

in his hand, "please make enough so that seconds will be as big as firsts."

Arieh sat in the shade of the tree with his daughter in his lap and kept the boys quiet with tales of past battles, while Dina bustled about preparing a meal and — for some reason — taking extra pains with it.

"Why do men have to kill each other?" Benjamin asked Arieh.

"I don't know," said Arieh. "I've never liked killing, but I know that if I weren't out there on guard with my spear in my hand, other men would be killing my family and my tribesmen. That's the way the world is, I guess."

"Oh, stop that solemn talk, you little owl," Dina said. "We're going to have a gay meal. Come and get it."

It was a gay meal, too, lots of jokes and laughter. And seconds were as big as firsts.

After that, the children were always coming around, especially at mealtimes. Arieh was always coming to take them away and he, too, would end up by staying a while.

One day, after Arieh and his children had left, Benjamin said to Dina, "You're practically mother to those children. You might as well be married to him."

"You shut your mouth, Benjamin son of Jacob," Dina flared at him and flounced off into her tent. She was back in a moment. She took her little brother in her arms and kissed him.

"Little darling," she said, "forgive me. I don't know what's the matter with me."

"Don't cry, Dina," said Benjamin. "Please don't cry."

"I don't know what's the matter with me," Dina repeated.

Benjamin had a little trouble persuading Jacob that Arieh and Dina should get married. At first, he refused to take it seriously. Then, he said it was impossible. Finally, he talked to Arieh.

"You do me great honor, chief," Arieh said. "I have loved your daughter for some time; but I never dared to aspire so high."

Dina, too, proved to be an unusually dutiful daughter when Jacob spoke to her about marrying Arieh.

"If it is my father's wish," she murmured with downcast eyes, "I shall be happy to obey."

None of the brothers objected to the marriage. Arieh was a good warrior, a respected member of the tribe and no one could find anything to say against him. The wedding was scheduled for the new moon.

Uzi accepted the coming marriage philosophically. He confided to Benjamin, "She's so bossy about washing and things like that, anyway, she might as well be my mother."

The wedding feast was as elaborate as befitted a chieftan's daughter. Jacob, as tribal leader, officiated at the ceremony and, as father of the bride, made a special sacrifice to God, with a prayer for the couple's happiness.

After the ceremony, Dina stood quite still as each of her brothers came up and kissed her. Reuben was the last to come up and, after a little hesitation, she returned his kiss.

Benjamin, of course, was too young to be a member of the tribe and was not permitted to participate in the ceremony. He stood on the outskirts of the assembled tribesmen with the other children, his eyes brimming with joy.

"Dear God," he prayed in his heart during the sacrifice, "Let Dina be happy, please. She's been unhappy for so long. And, dear God, make people understand that, if everybody loved everybody else, then everybody would be happy."

Chapter XI

Wedding celebrations followed the same pattern four thousand years ago very much as they do today. Once the religious formalities were gotten over with, the assembled guests started in seriously to liven up the party.

Wineskins were passed about, clay cups were filled, and the guests drank to the health of the bride. Then they drank to the health of the bridegroom. Then they drank to the health of the bride's parents. Then they drank to the health of the bridegroom's parents.

By the time they got around to drinking to the health of the bride's grandmother's twenty-second cousin, they were feeling pretty good. Somebody struck up a song and everyone joined in. Then another song and another.

The dancing started. Only the men danced. The women and young girls remained modestly seated — out of the way. The men danced around and around the roaring fire. After a while, the older men dropped out of the circle, leaving the center of the stage to the younger men—the prize warriors of the tribe.

How those young bucks strutted and whirled and leaped. The more active—and more daring—dancers leaped clean across the campfire, clearing the flickering flames by a fraction of an inch. Landing with a thud on the other side, they smiled slightly as the heard the gasps of admiration from the watching girls.

Benjamin caught a movement from the corner of his eye and turned to see. His father, seated in the place of honor, had put down the wine cup that he had barely tasted. He got up slowly. No one seemed to notice. Slowly, slowly, Jacob walked out of the circle of light into the shadws and then headed for his tent.

"Father isn't feeling well," thought Benjamin. "I can see the pain in his face and feel the pain in his heart."

He followed his father to his tent and went softly after him inside. Jacob was sitting on his couch. His face was hidden in his hands. No sound came from him.

"Father," said Benjamin quietly, "are you all right?"

Jacob started slightly and raised his head.

"I'm fine, son," he answered. "Why don't you go back to the party and enjoy yourself?"

"Come with me, father," said Benjamin. "They're just starting to serve the roast meat."

"Somehow," said Jacob, "I don't feel in the mood for celebrations. You go ahead without me, boy. We won't have a feast like that again for a long time. Go on, now."

"I'd rather stay here with you, father," said Benjamin, "unless you order me out of your tent."

"Order you out of my tent!" Jacob spluttered. "How you talk! Of course I won't order you out of my tent. I just can't understand why the youngest brother of the bride would pass up the wedding feast just to sit with a sad and lonely old man."

"Why do you feel sad and lonely, father?" Benjamin asked. "Aren't you glad that Dina is getting married?"

"Of course I am," said Jacob. "I'm very glad for her."

"Don't you approve of Arieh, father?"

"On the contrary. I've gotten to know him a little better, lately. He's a good man. In every way. One of the best we have in the tribe. I think he'll make Dina a good husband and that she'll be happy with him. High time, too. She's been miserable for a long time. Not all her fault, either."

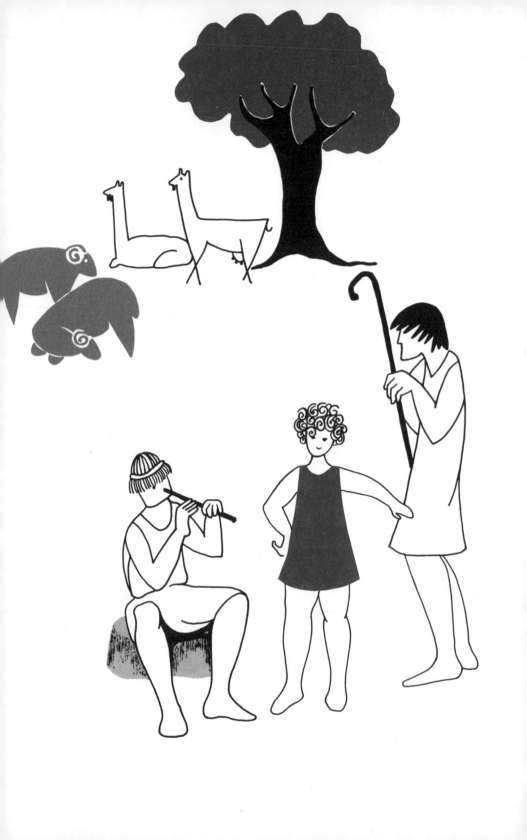

"Then," said Benjamin, "why, on this night of all nights, do you feel sad and lonely?"

"Questions, questions, questions," said Jacob testily. "You're just like your mother, God rest her soul. She was never satisfied until she knew what was in my heart. She'd keep on asking me until she found out."

Benjamin said nothing. After a moment, Jacob continued quietly, "I suppose that's why I'm feeling sad. As I sat there watching the festivities, I suddenly remembered our wedding and how she looked and I kept wishing she were sitting there beside me."

"Tell me about her, father," said Benjamin.

"I can't," Jacob answered. "I can't talk about Rachel, even after all these years. I'm sorry, son."

"Then tell me another story, father."

"Lord in heaven preserve me," Jacob groaned in mock despair, "I've told you a thousand stories and still you're not satisfied. I don't know any more stories. I've told you every one I know."

"No, father," said Benjamin, "A long time ago, you told me that God tested you and I asked you how and you said you'd tell me some time. You never told me, though. Would you tell me that story now?"

Jacob leaned back and closed his eyes. After a

while, a smile spread over his face and he chuckled reminiscently.

"That was a time," said Jacob with a light laugh. "Lord, that was a time."

"Tell me, father," said Benjamin eagerly. "Is it a funny story?" Jacob shook his head.

"It didn't seem funny at the time," he said. "In fact, I was just about scared out of my wits."

"Tell me! Tell me!"

"Just a moment, boy. Let me get it straight in my head. It was a long time ago." He remained for a long while sunk in thought. After what seemed like forever to Benjamin, he continued, "It was a long time ago. Before you were born. I had just run away from my father-in-law, Lavan."

"Why did you run away, father?"

"Because, if I had stayed, he would have killed me."

"Why did he want to kill you, father?"

"That's quite beside the point. I can only tell one story at a time. Do you want to hear the story about how God tested me or don't you?"

"Yes, please, father."

"Then stop interrupting me!"

"I won't do it again, father." Jacob looked at his youngest son, smiled and tousled his hair.

"Well, then. Where was I?"

"Lavan wanted to kill you."

"Oh, yes. Well, I got away from him all right thanks to your mother."

Benjamin said, "How...?" and then stopped himself.

"That's right," said Jacob. "That's another story entirely. Well, I wanted to get back to my father, who was camped in Hebron. And to do that I had to cross the Land of Seir."

"Was that bad, father?"

"Very bad, son. You see, the Land of Seir was ruled by my twin brother, Esau, who—last I heard—had sworn to kill me."

"What happened, father?"

"I had to cross his country. There was no other way open for us. I sent messengers to him with very polite greetings and some extremely expensive presents. My messengers came back to me and reported that Esau had taken the presents from them and had said no word, but he and two hundred of his fiercest warriors had mounted camels and were speeding toward me as fast as they could gallop."

"Oh," said Benjamin.

"Oh, indeed," answered Jacob. "You saw Esau, when you were a very little boy. I don't suppose you remember him. Anyway, Esau was capable of killing me and my family and then making a joke about it."

"What did you do, father?"

"I prayed to our God. I sent everyone across the river to camp and I stayed by myself in the wilderness and prayed to God."

"And God helped you?"

"He sent an angel to me."

"To fight Esau?"

"No," said Jacob smilingly, "to fight me." Benjamin's forehead crinkled. He was a very puzzled boy.

"I'm sorry, father," he finally said. "I just don't understand."

"I didn't either, at the time," Jacob said. "I saw the angel coming down from the sky and ran to meet him. By the time I got there, there was a man standing there. When I reached him, he attacked me savagely and tried to kill me."

"What did you do?" Benjamin asked breathlessly.

"I fought back," Jacob answered. "He was strong, but I was just as strong. He fought hard, but I fought just as hard. We fought all night and then, as the sun was rising, he said to me: Let me go now, it will soon be morning. And I said: I won't let you go until you tell me who you are and why you tried to kill me."

"What did he say?"

"He said: What is you name? and I said: Jacob. And he said: From today onward, your name is Israel. Because you fought the power of heaven and were not beaten.

"And I called to him: Wait a moment. What do you mean? What are you trying to say? He said to me : You fought an angel and he could not beat you. Will you be afraid of a man, today? And he was gone!"

"What a strange story," said Benjamin, "Is there more to it?"

"Yes," said Jacob. "I crossed the river into camp. I had been fighting the angel for a good many hours and had hurt my leg pretty badly in the fight, so that I was limping. But, strangely enough, I didn't feel tired and — what was more important — I didn't feel frightened. I ordered the tents struck and we rode forward to meet Esau."

"And what did Esau do, father?"

"Nothing much. We talked over old times and joked together. I gave him one or two practical suggestions for his business dealings. He was — and is — a very successful caravan robber. We parted good friends. Now, do you see the point of the story?"

"I'm not sure, father," Benjamin said.

"I don't know if you remember," said Jacob, "but a long time ago I told you that God tests us, not to find out what we will do because He knows what we will do. He tests us to show us what we can do. And when we pass His tests, we conquer fear and doubt. That's the point. Do you see it, son?"

"Yes, father," Benjamin said. "Thank you for the story."

"Thank you, son, for staying with a sad and lonely old man, who," Jacob added with some surprise, "no longer feels sad and lonely, for some reason or other. Story telling is thirsty work. I wonder if there's any wine left. Shall we go see?"

"Maybe we can find something left to eat, too," Benjamin smiled.

Hand in hand, father and son, walked out of the tent to rejoin the merrymaking wedding guests.

Chapter XII

The tribe finally reached Beer Sheba. She was a sadly neglected city, the city of the seven wells, the Queen City of the Desert, that Abraham had founded. In fact, she had sunk to nothing but a way station on the caravan route.

Jacob came to an understanding with the local people and the tribe settled in Beer Sheba without incident. It was different now than it had been in Abraham's time.

At that time, the tribe had been small and unknown. Every time Abraham and his people had dug a well, the local inhabitants had either filled it in or refused to let them use it. Six wells they dug, and six times the well they had worked so hard for had been taken away from them.

It was not until the Philistine king, Abimelech, stepped in and came to an agreement with Abraham that the little tribe had been allowed to live in peace and the seventh well that they dug remained theirs. The grove of trees that Abraham had planted still stood.

Now, things were different. The tribe was large and had a reputation in the land. It had many warriors and at their head stood the ten stalwart sons of Jacob. No, the surrounding tribes would think twice before attacking the tribe of Israel.

Benjamin had a wonderful time walking around the city with his father and listening to him tell of its history. History is one thing when you read about it in a book. It's quite another thing when you're walking in the place where it happened.

Once the tribe had settled in, the routine of work

began. The flocks had to be fed and watered. The crops had to be planted and harvested. Wresting a living from the desert has never been easy.

If the flocks grew fat and increased and if the crops succeeded — man lived. If not, he died of starvation. That was — and is — the iron law of the desert. In addition, man had to defend the fruits of his labor from those who thought it was easier to take what someone else had worked for than to work for it themselves.

Benjamin was considered big enough to go to work now. The chief's sons worked as hard as anyone else. Idleness is a luxury that desert dwellers cannot afford. Every pair of working hands was precious to the tribe.

Young Benjamin was assigned to work as apprentice shepherd with his brothers Gad and Asher. At first, the two older brothers were inclined to be stand-offish and surly; but who could resist Benjamin?

His love just poured forth and they could not help smiling back at him. He was so sunny and cheerful. His laugh was so infectious. Besides, he was a willing worker, always trying to do just a little more than his share. After a few weeks of working together with him, Gad and Asher — who

82

had never had much to do with their littlest brother — loved Benjamin as much as everyone did.

During the long afternoons, when the sheep were resting and there was nothing much to do, Asher would teach Benjamin to play the shepherd's pipes; or they would talk. Benjamin was a good listener and, before his older brothers knew it, they were telling Benjamin all about the hurt and resentment in their hearts.

"It's all right for you," said Gad. "Not that we have anything against you personally, Benjamin, but your mother was one of father's wives. We're sons of a concubine and it makes a difference."

"Gad, you're talking way over the boy's head," said Asher. "He doesn't even known what a concubine is. Do you, Benjamin?" Benjamin shook his head.

"Well, look," said Asher. "You know that some men have more than one wife, don't you?" Benjamin nodded.

"You see," said Asher, "a man can have as many wives as he wants — if he can support them. But wives are from families that are his social equals. If a man wants to marry a girl who's his social inferior — a slave girl — for instance, he doesn't have to go through a wedding ceremony. Do you understand?"

"And," Gad added bitterly, "she's called a concubine, not a wife. And a son of a chief's concubine can never become head of the tribe. Unless the chief's wives don't have any sons. Or the sons all die."

"Or," said Asher meaningfully, "the concubine's son kills all the other sons."

"And your mother was father's concubine?" Benjamin asked.

"One of them," said Gad. "Father had two wives and two concubines. Didn't he ever tell you?"

'No," said Benjamin.

"You spend enough time with him," said Asher. "What do you talk about?"

"God, mostly," said Benjamin.

"Oh, that," Gad said, "Well, father's a holy man, right enough. But didn't he ever tell you about when he was at Uncle Lavan's?"

"No," said Benjamin. "Only that he went to Uncle Lavan's because Esau wanted to kill him."

"Ah, there was a city," said Asher, "Padan, in the land of Haran. That's where Uncle Lavan lived It was bigger than Beer Sheba and Hebron combined. Remember the fun we used to have in the bazars, Gad?"

"Stick to the point, Asher," Gad said. "Well, father came to Uncle Lavan's and the first thing he saw was Rachel, Lavan's daughter, and he fell in love with her."

"But he didn't have the bridal price," continued Asher. "You know what bridal price is, don't you?"

"When Arieh wanted to marry Dina, I heard them talking about it," said Benjamin, "but I didn't really understand what it is."

"Well, look," Gad said, "you want to marry a girl, see. So your father goes to her father and they talk about it. If they come to an agreement, your father pays her father the bridal price in gold or silver or camels or sheep, whatever. Do you understand, Benjamin?"

"And the prettier the girl and the better her family, the higher the bridal price is," explained Asher.

Benjamin's brows knitted in thought as he said, "If a boy and a girl love each other and want to get married, why can't they do it without this business of fathers and families and bridal price?"

Asher and Gad looked at each other and burst out laughing.

"Benjamin, you say the darndest things," chuckled Gad. "Things just aren't done that way, that's all."

"What about father wanting to get married and not having the bridal price?" said Benjamin.

"Well," said Asher, "he agreed to work for Uncle Lavan for seven years so that he could marry Rachel."

"And did he?" asked Benjamin.

"Oh, that Lavan was a shrewd one," chuckled Gad. "At the end of seven years, he got father drunk at the wedding feast and when he woke up in the morning he found that he had married — not Rachel — but her older sister, Leah!"

Chapter XIII

That set off Asher and Gad into a laughing fit. They lay back on the ground and roared with laughter so hard that tears squirted from their eyes. Their bellowing startled the sheep and Benjamin had to go among them and make soothing noises to them to get them to lie down again.

When Benjamin got back to Asher and Gad, they were both sitting up. Asher was shaking his head and wiping his eyes, while Gad was trying to stop hiccuping long enough to take a drink from the goatskin water bag.

"Uncle Lavan doesn't sound like a nice person," Benjamin said.

"Nice," chortled Asher. "He could steal the teeth from your mouth while you weren't looking and then, when you turned around, he could sell them back to you at double the market price. Oh, it was a pleasure to watch him at work. He knew how to live, too."

Gad had by this time succeeded in getting a drink of water and overcoming his hiccups. He wiped his mouth with his hand and said, "Ah, those were the days. You missed all that, Benjamin, getting born so late."

"So how did father finally get to marry Rachel?" Benjamin asked.

"He had to work another seven years for Uncle Lavan to earn the bridal price for her," said Asher, "that's how."

"But I still don't understand..."

"Look, Benjamin," said Gad. "Father married Leah. She bore him six sons — Reuben, Simeon, Levi, Judah and Issachar and — and — "

"Zebulon," prompted Asher.

"Oh, yes, Zebulon," said Gad, "and one daughter, Dina. Got that straight?"

"Yes," said Benjamin.

"Bright boy," said Gad. "Then father married Rachel and she had two boys, Joseph and you. Still following me?"

"Yes," said Benjamin.

"Now," said Gad, "your mother had a slave girl for her handmaiden. Her name was Bilhah. She bore father two sons — Dan and Naphtali. She was a concubine. Understand that?" Benjamin nodded.

"Leah had a slave girl for a handmaiden, too. Her name was Zilpah. She became father's concubine, too. She was our mother — Asher's and mine."

"I remember her," said Benjamin. "She was always very kind to me when I was a little boy."

"By all the demons of the desert," Asher burst forth, "Why did she have to be a concubine? Why couldn't she have been a wife? Then the others wouldn't have been able to lord it over us all these years !"

"Asher, Asher," said Benjamin, "why do you torture yourself like that?"

"Because I won't be a slave to them !" grated Asher. "The chief is my father, too, and I'm as good as any of them!"

"You see, Benjamin," said Gad, "as long as Joseph was alive and it was plain that he was father's favorite, we were all together on one thing: we hated Joseph. But now that we've got Joseph out of the way..."

"Shut your big mouth," said Asher warningly.

"Because of his unfortunate death by accident," Gad continued smoothly, "the question comes up — who's going to be chief of the tribe when father dies?"

"Why, Reuben is," said Benjamin. "He's the oldest."

Asher and Gad smiled at each other meaningfully. Asher shook his head and included Benjamin in his smile. "No, little brother, not Reuben. He's weak as water."

"He is not," said Benjamin hotly. "He's strong and brave!"

"Oh, he's a good warrior, all right," said Gad, "I'll grant you that. But in the fight for the chieftanship, he won't stand a chance. No, it's between Simeon, Judah and Levi. Judah is the strongest. Simeon has got a will of iron and Levi is the smartest. I should say, the slyest. It will be an interesting fight to watch."

"I won't just stand by and watch," said Asher, "I won't serve under any of them."

"If Dan and Naphtali would only join us," said Gad, "we could..."

"Will you shut your big mouth," said Asher in exasperation.

"Oh, shut your own," said Gad belligerently.

"Do you realize whom you're talking to?" asked Asher.

"I'm talking to Benjamin," said Gad. "Have you ever heard Benjamin going around blabbing any secrets? I haven't. And I'll bet he knows plenty. Don't you. Benjamin? Benjamin shrugged and kept silent.

"See what I mean?" said Gad. "Now, if Benjamin would only join us..."

"Benjamin's a child," said Asher.

"He won't always be," retorted Gad. "Boys become men. If Benjamin would join us, Dan and Naphtali would, too. Then we'd stand a chance against the others."

"Would you join us, Benjamin?" Asher asked slowly.

"Join you in what?" Benjamin asked.

"Look, Benjamin," said Asher urgently, "you're one of father's legitimate sons. If you could get him to bestow the chieftanship upon you, we four would serve under you and back you against the others."

"Suppose the others object? asked Benjamin.

"Then we'd fight them," said Gad.

"Shed our brothers' blood !" said Benjamin, aghast.

"The blood guilt would be upon them, not upon

us," said Asher. "We'd be carrying out our father's wishes. They'd be the rebels."

"Suppose they win?" said Benjamin.

"Then we'll be dead and won't have anything to worry about," said Gad matter-of-factly. "And if we win, they'll be dead and they won't have anything to worry about."

"Why?" asked Benjamin desperately, "Why must we kill each other? Why can't we live in peace?"

"Because we're men," said Asher. "And we won't be slaves. Are you joining us, Benjamin?"

"I can't," said Benjamin. "Even if I wanted to. I can't kill."

"We'll do the killing," said Gad.

"I can't join you in a thing like this," said Benjamin, "I can't and I won't."

Asher looked at Gad. Gad shrugged. Asher said to him, "You should have kept your mouth shut, Gad. I warned you." Gad shrugged again.

"I took a chance," he admitted. "It was a chance worth taking."

"Benjamin, you know too much now," Asher said. "Either you're with us or you're against us. And if you're against us, you disappear. Now."

"You mean you'd kill me," said Benjamin.

"We like you, Benjamin," said Asher. "We like

you very much. But we like our necks better. We can't take a chance on your repeating what we've just said."

"I won't betray you," said Benjamin.

"We can't take the chance," said Asher. "Are you with us?"

"No," said Benjamin. "Go ahead and kill me."

Asher stood irresolute for a few minutes, then he turned to Gad and said, "Gad, you do it." Gad slowly shook his head.

"I can't," he said.

"I can't either," said Asher. "We'll just have to take the chance. And if we're going to get these sheep back by dark, we'll have to get a move on. Come on, you dumb brutes, move! Move!"

Chapter XIV

Benjamin was a big boy now and everybody was saying it was time he got married. Children got married early in those days. Boys were considered eligible bachelors at fifteen or sixteen. Girls started getting offers of marriage at fourteen — or, rather, their fathers did.

To this very day, among Arabs and Jews coming

from Oriental countries, what we would call "Child marriages" are not uncommon. It is not unusual for a bachelor of thirty to marry a girl of fourteen.

At any rate, interest in the tribe was pretty high: whom would Benjamin, the chief's youngest son, marry? Mothers with marriageable daughters among the leading families of the tribe began talking to their husbands. Their husbands (after telling their wives not to bother them, they had more important things to think about) began sending representatives to Jacob.

Jacob listened courteously to all offers, asked the men to thank their masters for their offers, and said he would consider the matter. He called his son to him and said, "Benjamin, my dear boy, have you thought of getting married?"

"Frankly, no, father," Benjamin answered.

"It is our duty to be fruitful and multiply, to increase the tribe," Jacob said, "God himself has commandedi t. Isn't there anyone you love?"

"I love everyone, father."

"Yes, yes, I know," Jacob smiled. "But isn't there any particular girl you fancy?"

"No, father," Benjamin said.

"Well, think about it, son," Jacob said. "Look around and make your choice. There isn't a family in the tribe that wouldn't be glad to have you for a son-in-law. So choose a bride, son. Take your time, but don't be too long about it."

News of the conversation got about. It was pretty hard to keep a secret in the close-knit life of the tribe. Interest mounted higher. Benjamin went about his everyday work, answering all joking from the men of the tribe with his usual smile. He was unfailingly polite to the mothers who engaged him in conversations on the subject — but he didn't commit himself. The girls watched, and whispered together, and giggled excitedly.

Some time went by and, since Benjamin made no move to reopen the subject of his marriage, Jacob called him to his tent again.

"Benjamin, my son," Jacob began, "you remember our conversation of some time ago —- about your getting married?"

"Yes, father," Benjamin answered.

"Well, have you come to any decision, boy?" Jacob asked a little impatiently. "Have you chosen a bride?"

"Yes, father," Benjamin said, "I should like to marry Deborah.

"Deborah? Deborah? Which Deborah? I don't remember getting any offers from any family with a girl named Deborah."

"We didn't get any offer, father," Benjamin said.

"I want to ask you to make an offer to her father, Arieh."

"Which Arieh?" asked Jacob in genuine puzzlement.

"The Arieh who married your daughter, Dina."

"That Arieh," said Jacob. "But, good heavens boy, he's nobody!"

"He's a member of the tribe of Israel," said Benjamin quietly.

"Yes, of course," said Jacob, feeling that the rebuke was justified. "I had hoped for a more important connection for you."

"You asked me to choose, father," said Benjamin. "I have chosen. If you want to make another choice for me, I shall obey your will, of course."

"No, no, Benjamin," said Jacob testily, "I won't force you in a matter like this. God forbid. I have nothing against the match. I have nothing to say in favor of it," he added with a smile, "but you shall have your wish. I'll send someone to talk to Arieh tomorrow."

"Thank you," said Benjamin. "Good night, my father."

"It used to be a lot harder to get you to say 'Good night' not so long ago. You used to keep me up till all hours telling you stories. Remember?"

"I remember, father," Benjamin said. "Your stories are part of my fondest memories."

"Only yesterday, you were a little boy begging for stories. And now, you're a young man about to get married. Lord, Lord, how time flies," Jacob sighed. "Well, good night, dearest Benjamin. May our God bless you and give you a happy life. Good night."

Arieh was overwhelmed when he received Jacob's offer. He was an ordinary warrior from a humble family of the tribe of Israel. Not only had he married the chief's daughter, but now his daughter was going to marry the chief's son! God had indeed been good to him. He accepted the honor with expressions of pleasure and gratitude.

The news spread through the tribe like wildfire. Most people laughed. Some, more thoughtful, wondered why Benjamin had chosen as he did. Mothers with marriageable daughters were indignant. Their own precious jewel of a daughter passed over in favor of that ugly, little nobody, Deborah! Well! People had always said that the chief's youngest son was a little soft in the head. A person could very well believe it!

Dina came to see Benjamin and she didn't beat about the bush. She looked Benjamin squarely in the eye and said, "Little brother, I want to know why. Now, Deborah is my daughter — don't you smile at me, monkey face, I don't make any difference between Arieh's children, whether I bore them or whether his first wife did. Deborah is my daughter and I know what a fine girl she is. But the truth is the truth. She's plain and her family is not very distinguished. You could have had the most beautiful girl of the finest family in the tribe for your wife. What made you choose Deborah? Do you love her?"

"I love everyone. Now, wait, Dina," Benjamin said as Dina opened her mouth to interrupt, "I know what you're going to say. Don't bother. Has Deborah received any other offers of marriage?"

"No," said Dina. "And I doubt if she would have received any. That's the point."

"Yes, dear sister," said Benjamin. "That's the point. I know Deborah. We were playmates when we were children."

"I don't understand what you're trying to say," said Dina.

"I'm trying to say that when someone I know is hurt and humiliated, I can't bear the pain. Deborah was scorned by all of the young men of the tribe. I felt her pain and shame. I couldn't bear it."

Dina's eyes shone as she said to him softly, "A

long time ago, I said that there was no one like you in the world, little brother. I say it again."

"I'll walk with you to your tent, big sister," Benjamin smiled at her.

As he was returning, a voice called to him from the shadows. As he approached the dim figure, he saw that it was Deborah.

"Deborah," he said softly. "What are you doing out here? Don't you know it's forbidden for the groom to see the bride before the wedding?" Deborah fell upon her knees and kissed Benjamin's hand.

"Oh, my lord," she said, her eyes brimming with tears. "My lord."

He raised her gently to her feet and kissed her, saying, "Stop this 'my lord' nonsense, Deborah. I used to give you camel rides on my back. Now, run along home or people won't stop talking about the scandal for the next fifty years."

"You won't be sorry you married me," said Deborah, her voice husky with emotion, "I'll be a good wife to you."

"I know you will, Deborah," said Benjamin, winking at her. "That's why I picked you."

Chapter XV

The greatest similarity between the man of four thousand years ago and the man of today is that if man doesn't eat for any length of time, he dies. And death by starvation is one of the most horrible ways to die.

Hunger is still a human problem today. Four thousand years ago, famine was feared more than the most relentless human foe. Because man saw famine as a punishment of mysterious and implacable gods. And if his prayers and his sacrifices upon the altars didn't help, nothing did. He and his children were doomed to death by starvation. Small wonder that famine produced panic of epidemic proportions.

About a year after Benjamin's marriage, famine struck the land of Canaan. The first thing a migratory tribe did when there was no food in one place was to pack up and go to another place where there was food.

The reports that Jacob received as tribal leader, however, showed that there was no place to go. The entire land of Canaan was in the relentless and dreaded grip of famine.

The tribe began to suffer from hunger. You couldn't keep slaughtering sheep and goats and cattle for food. That was living off your capital and only put off starvation for a while. Man needed bread to eat if he wanted to go on living.

As the famine got worse, the beasts of prey of the desert became more desperate and daring. Weakened by hunger, the shepherds had to fight off their attacks on the herds and flocks. It's hard to be alert and active when your belly is growling because it's empty.

The grumblings of dissatisfaction became outcries of protest. All of it was directed at Jacob. He was the tribal leader. Why didn't he do something? That is the most terrible position for a responsible man to be in. Your people demand that you "do something". And you don't know what to do!

It was a very bad time for Benjamin. Sensitive as he was to the suffering of others, to see children crying because they were hungry and to see their mothers crying because they had no food to give them was sheer agony.

The agony mounted and grew as time went on. Children — and grownups — began dying of starvation. The silence of the dead and the wailing of the living mourners cut deep into Benjamin's heart.

He would give away his food to hungry children until his wife, Deborah caught him at it. After that, she would corner him in their tent and practically force-feed him with whatever she could scrounge at least once every two days.

Benjamin went to his father to plead with him to "do something" to alleviate the hunger of the people. Jacob, his nerves frayed by the responsibility of a crisis, spoke angrily to his youngest son for the first time.

"Stop whining at me, you whey-faced milksop," he blazed at Benjamin. "Do you think I don't know how bad things are? Do you think I'm blind and deaf? Do you think I haven't been racking my brains to think of something to do? If you don't have any advice, don't come to me with complaints! Get out of here and let me think."

The sharp, bitter words hurt Benjamin more because they were so unexpected and so unusual. His father had never before spoken unkindly to him. Very few people had. Benjamin sent forth love and got back love. He overcame his shock and hurt and persisted.

"Dear father," he said softly, "forgive me for adding to your troubles. But I must speak, I can't keep still. God has appeared to you and spoken to you. He promised you the land of Canaan. He said that our people would be a great nation, as numerous as the sands of the seashore and as uncountable as the stars in the sky. What has happened to that promise? How can we be a great nation if we all die here of hunger. And we are dying. One by one. Soon, we'll all be dead. Father, speak to God."

"Do you think I haven't tried?" asked Jacob bitterly, his face bleak.

"And what happened?"

"God didn't answer me," said Jacob sombrely, "We are lost."

"No, father, no," said Benjamin urgently, "I don't believe our God would abandon us. Don't lose hope. I'm sure God will send you the wisdom to save us."

When he left his father's tent, Benjamin walked out into the desert under the stars. He looked up at the jewel-studded sky.

"God of my fathers," Benjamin whispered, "I love you. Even if you kill us. I love you."

Benjamin's ten older brothers would have taken advantage of the rebellious unrest against their father's rule. Each one of them kept thinking how to turn the situation to his own advantage. None

104

of them could think of anything. They didn't know what to do, either.

They were surprised, and a little uneasy, when they received a summons from their father to meet in his tent. None of them had as yet done anything outright, but guilty thoughts make for a guilty conscience.

When they had all assembled, Jacob addressed them. He spoke soberly, yet his voice had a ring of confidence. He looked at each of them in turn as he said, "My sons, you are going to save the tribe."

"How?" asked Reuben.

"There is bread in Egypt. You will go down to Egypt and buy some."

There was babel of sound from the assembled brothers. Levi's voice pierced through the others, "How do you know there's bread in Egypt? And even if there is, who knows if they'll sell us any?"

"God knows," said Jacob quietly. "He told me to send you."

That seemed to settle it. The brothers looked at one another. Judah asked, "Whom are you sending?"

"You ten," said Jacob.

"What about Benjamin?" Asher asked.

"I've lost one of Rachel's sons," said Jacob, "I'm not endangering the other one. Benjamin stays here."

Chapter XVI

The entire tribe turned out to see the brothers start off to Egypt. Each brother's face was set and sober. Each was fully aware of the great responsibility that rested on his shoulders.

If they returned from Egypt with corn, their people would live. If they failed in their mission, their people would die. The fate of the tribe was in their hands. Their families and friends depended upon them.

They all fussed with the harnesses of the pack donkeys they were taking with them to carry back the corn. They were nervous and their fingers fumbled. They kicked and cursed at the donkeys who brayed in protest.

Finally, Reuben at the head of the line gave the ringing drawn-out call to start. The donkeys, urged on by whip and word, started. The brothers set their stern faces southward and began the long, fateful journey to Egypt.

Their wives, tearful but proud of them, waved after them. Their children, hungry but proud of their fathers, called after them to hurry home. The tribal chief, their father, raised his hands in blessing. Benjamin looked longingly after them. He would have liked to go with his brothers on their dangerous journey. It would have been easier than this waiting and watching his tribesmen suffering.

The days turned into weeks and there was no sign of the brothers' return. The people began to despair. Jacob had given up hoping a week ago and secretly mourned his sons. Only Benjamin still believed that God would not forsake them, that He would bring the brothers back safely — and with food for the hungry tribe.

One day, the lookout raised a shout, "There they are!" Everyone rushed to the top of the hill. There, far off in the desert, tiny specks were moving toward them. The keen eyed desert dwellers could already make out that the spots were men and donkeys moving across the sands.

"God be praised," said one of the women. "All ten of them, back safe and sound."

"The donkeys are heavily laden," said one of the men, "I can see that. And... just a moment ! I can only see nine men! Is my counting wrong?"

Anxiously, the more keen eyed began counting the men. Yes, the first man had been right. Ten brothers had set out. Only nine were returning! Who was missing?

As the men came nearer and it was possible to distinguish between them, the tense identification began. That was Reuben in the lead, all right. That was Levi and that was Judah, no mistaking him. Who was missing?

As all of the brothers were identified, one family set up a wailing. Simeon was missing. His children gathered about their mother crying. His wife tearfully tried to comfort them.

As the brothers came up, Reuben's first words were to Simeon's family. He called to them, "Don't cry. Simeon is alive and well. He remained behind in Egypt." A babel of questions rose up.

"I'll tell you all about it after you've eaten," Rebuen shouted over the noise, "Now line up, everyone. We're going to start measuring out the corn. Don't crowd. There's enough for everybody."

Jacob watched the whole proceeding, stone-faced. When the brothers came up to greet him, he said sternly, "Who told you to give out the corn, Reuben? Who told you how much to give out? I thought I was still chief of this tribe!"

"What kind of a man are you?" Judah burst forth,

"We've just come back from a long and dangerous trip with bread to save the lives of our people. Simeon, your son, is still in prison in that accursed land. Who knows if we'll ever see him alive again. And what do you worry about? Who measures out the corn! Are you made of stone, old man?"

Benjamin stepped in hastily. He said soothingly, "Peace, my brothers. Father spoke like that because he has been half out of his mind with worry for you. Father, forgive Judah's rude speech. You can see for yourself how worn and tired your brave sons are. Why don't we all go to our tents now to eat and rest. This evening, we'll have a thanksgiving service to our Lord who brought you back safely and we'll hear your story."

The brothers agreed and dispersed grumbling. Jacob entered his tent without a word. Benjamin went over and helped the men unload the donkeys and store the corn. Then they gave the donkeys water and turned them out to pasture.

That night, before a great roaring fire, the tribe watched Jacob go through the ritual of thanksgiving to God. Jacob finished and then took his seat, calling upon the brothers to tell of their adventures.

Reuben rose and said, "When we got to Egypt, we found people from all over the land of Canaan and its neighboring lands in Egypt. The Egyptians were selling corn and we got into a line of buyers with our sacks and our money in our hands."

"As soon as the Egyptian governor saw us," Levi continued, "he accused us of being spies. We protested that we were honest men, come to Egypt to buy corn like everybody else. He wouldn't listen to us and threw us all in jail."

"It took a whole squad of their piddling police to do it," growled Judah, "but into the dungeon we all went. And we stayed there for three days. Then they let us out."

"Then what happened?" Jacob asked.

"That Egyptian governor asked us a lot of questions," Reuben said. "Strange questions, some of them. Did we have a younger brother at home? Was our father still alive and well?"

"How he knew about us," said Levi, "we couldn't for the life of us figure out. Anyway, he said he'd let us buy corn if we'd bring our younger brother with us next time. Then he said he'd keep Simeon in jail until we brought him our younger brother."

"We paid him our money," Reuben took up the story, "and they weighed out the corn and put them in the sacks. We started back and, when I opened a sack to feed the donkeys some corn, there was the money I had paid. All the others opened their sacks and they, too, found their money with the corn."

"What did this governor look like?" Benjamin asked.

"He looked like an Egyptian," said Judah. "What would he look like?"

"What was his name?" Benjamin asked.

"Some Egyptian name," said Judah. "Who can pronounce it!"

"I can," said Dan quietly, "It was Zaphnath-paaneah. Why do you ask, Benjamin?"

"I just wondered," said Benjamin.

"He won't let Simeon out of jail," said Judah, looking at Jacob, "until we bring him Benjamin." Jacob looked straight ahead of him.

"I'm not sending Benjamin to Egypt," he said, tight-lipped. "And that's that!"

Chapter XVII

When the corn that the brothers had brought from Egypt was gone, Jacob ordered them to go to Egypt to buy more. The brothers refused to go without Benjamin. Jacob was rocklike in his refusal to let Benjamin go.

"Then keep your precious Benjamin by your side," said Reuben heatedly, "And watch us all starve to death before your eyes."

Benjamin himself joined his brothers in pleading with his father for permission to go. Finally, as the tribe began to suffer from hunger once again, Jacob relented and gave his permission with great misgiving.

Once again, a caravan of pack donkeys was quickly formed and a double amount of money was taken to pay for the last purchase of corn for which, somehow, the money had been returned.

Once again, ten of Jacob's sons set forth on the southward trek to Egypt. This time, the tenth son was Benjamin. Simeon was still in prison in the land of the Nile. The prayers, good wishes, and cries of encouragement followed the brothers long after they were out of earshot.

The journey passed uneventfully, though Benjamin's eyes feasted on sights that he had never seen or imagined. They reached Egypt and tried to take their places in the buyers' line as inconspicuously as possible. To no avail, there was that cursed Egyptian governor, Zaphnath-paaneah, sitting up on a high platform superintending the sales.

No sooner did his eye light upon the brothers, then he began giving orders and officials and guards began running in all directions. A captain of the guard came up to them and said politely, "Will you please follow me?"

"They're not putting me in that dungeon again," growled Judah, "Come on, brothers, we fight now!"

"Wait a minute, Judah," said Levi. "If they wanted to put us in jail, they wouldn't send one man. They know it took sixty guards to de it last time. Besides, the jail is over that way. This feathered cockatoo is asking us to follow him in the opposite direction."

"That's right, brothers," Reuben said. "Time enough to fight when we have to. Let's go along peaceably and see what happens." They followed the captain through the streets until they stopped in front of a beautifully ornate mansion. The captain motioned for them to enter.

"Just a moment," said Reuben. "What is this place?"

"Why, this is the home of the Honorable Governor, Zaphnath-paaneah," said the captain, pitying their ignorance. "His Honor's orders are that you are to enter."

At that moment, Simeon, accompanied by two guards, came in view from the opposite side of the street. He broke into a run and embraced his brothers.

"I'm all right," Simeon replied, in response to his brothers' questions, "I feel fine. It wasn't a bad jail, as jails go. Funny thing, though, there was an old convict there, been there all his life. I made friends with him and he told me they had another Hebrew in that jail a long time ago. He couldn't remember his name and he couldn't remember what happened to him. All he could remember was that he used to interpret dreams. He was disappointed I couldn't do it. He thought all Hebrews were able to interpret dreams."

There was an uneasy silence among the brothers. Reuben finally broke it by saying, "Well, let's go in and see what the Egyptian wants of us this time."

The door was opened by the Egyptian governor's overseer. Reuben tried to explain about the mixup with the money, but the overseer merely smiled and waved them inside. Standing on a dias above them, the governor spoke to them through an interpreter. He bade them welcome and inquired after the health of their father. He looked long and hard at Benjamin and then abruptly left the room.

The overseer invited the brothers to sit down to a banquet the like of which they had never seen. Half starved as they were, the brothers did not need a second invitation. The table was laden with more than enough food for fifty men, but there wasn't very much left by the time the brothers leaned back in their chairs with satisfied smiles on their faces.

During the time the brothers had been eating, the Egyptian governor had come back into the room and sat down at his own table. Egyptians didn't eat with barbarians. Benjamin looked at him and thought, "Why, he's been crying! He's washed his face to hide the traces of the tears, but I can see. He's been crying. Why? Why?"

At the end of the feast, the Egyptian governor, again speaking through an interpreter, said that if they would pay their money to his overseer, they would receive the sacks of corn all weighed out. He bade them farewell and wished them a pleasant journey.

They were leading their laden pack donkeys out of the city gates in less time than it takes to tell. After about a mile, they heaved a collective sigh of relief.

"Well, I'm willing to admit I was mistaken," said Judah."He wasn't a bad fellow, the Egyptian dog."

"It's not too late to change your mind," said Levi bitterly. "Look behind us!"

Judah looked. About a hundred Egyptian chariots were pursuing them. The brothers looked at one another. They were brave warriors, but there is a difference between bravery and suicidal mania. When the Egyptian chariots reached them, they surrendered without a struggle. Egyptian chariots had long knives on their wheels that could cut a man in two while passing him. It was a particularly messy way to die. The brothers surrendered and went back with the Egyptian soldiers.

Once more they faced the Egyptian governor. He was in a towering rage.

"What kind of men are you?" he asked indignantly through an interpreter, "I treated you well, didn't I?"

"Excellently well, your Lordship," said Reuben bowing. All the other brothers, bowed, too.

"Then why did you have to go and steal my silver goblet?" shouted the governor.

"Your Honor," said Reuben calmly, "last time we were here, you called us spies. This time you call us thieves. We cannot understand why you persecute us. We are humble folk, sheepherders, but we are honest men — neither spies nor thieves. If you find that one of us has stolen your silver goblet, you may kill him on the spot."

The guards opened the sacks and the goblet was found — in Benjamin's sack.

"I take you at your word," said the Egyptian coldly. "The boy dies."

There were four guards standing in front of the governor. Judah knocked them aside with one sweep of his arm.

"Your Honor," he said, kneeling and clasping the governor's robe, "I stole the goblet and put it in the boy's sack. Kill me. Kill all of us, but let the boy go home. We promised our father we would bring him home safely. If anything happens to him, our aged father will die of grief."

The other brothers added their entreaties to those of Judah, creating quite an uproar. A contingent of household guards came in on the run, their spears at the ready. Surprisingly enough, the Egyptian governor held up his hand to them in a command to halt.

In the ensuing quiet, Benjamin said, "My brothers, you are older than I am but you are acting like foolish children. Look at this man's face. It is not the face of an evil man. He means us no harm. I think I know who he is."

The Egyptian governor gave a harsh command. All Egyptians, guards and officials, left the room.

The Egyptian, Zaphnath-paaneah, turned to Benjamin and said, in Hebrew, "Who am I?"

In answer, Benjamin threw himself into his arms,

and the two embraced. Raising his tear-wet eyes to the other brothers, Zaphnath-paaneah said to them, "I am your brother, Joseph."

Chapter XVIII

With his brothers gathered about him, Joseph told them how he had been sold as a slave to an Egyptian official, Potiphar. How he had risen to the post of overseer in Potiphar's household. How Potiphar's wife had induced the official to throw Joseph into jail, where he had remained for some years.

Joseph told his brothers how he had come to the attention of the Pharaoh because of his ability to interpret dreams. He had interpreted a dream which had been troubling Pharaoh, which not one of Pharaoh's retinue of priests, necromancers and magicians had been able to interpret.

As a result, he had risen high in Pharaoh's service and was now second only to Pharaoh himself in the land of Egypt. Joseph introduced his brothers to his wife, Asenath, a beautiful and gracious Egyptian lady who had been the daughter of the Chief Priest of On. He showed them his two sturdy sons. Manasseh and Ephraim.

"My brothers," said Joseph, "let us not talk of the past. What has been is gone and is forgotten. Let us talk of the future. This famine will run for another five years. I want our father here where I can provide for him. Bring the whole tribe here to Egypt and I'll settle you all in the Land of Goshen. That's right on the border. You'll have no trouble leaving and going back to the land of Canaan once the famine is over."

When Jacob heard that his beloved son, Joseph, was not dead, but was a very high official in Egypt and wanted him to come to him, he wept for joy. He wanted very much to see his son before he died, but he was an old man and set in his ways. To pick up and move again, this time as far as Egypt, seemed to be too much.

However, when God appeared to him again and told him to go, that He would be with the Children of Israel and see to it that they returned once again to the land of Canaan, Jacob gave orders to strike tents and move.

Imagine the reunion between father and long-lost son when the tribe finally got to Egypt! Joseph had enough influence to see to it that Jacob was welcomed to Egypt with all the pomp and circumstance of a visiting dignitary. He was even able to arrange a reception with Pharaoh, who was very gracious to Jacob and never showed a trace of the condescension he must have felt for this barbaric chieftan.

The tribe settled down in the land of Goshen and stayed there even after the famine passed. Things were going well. Why should they leave?

Jacob died, in the fullness of his years, and was buried in the land of Canaan. On his deathbed, he had blessed all of his sons and had strictly enjoined them not to let his bones lie in Egypt, but to take them to the burying place of his fathers in the field of Machpelah near Hebron.

Joseph had his father's body embalmed by the best embalmers in Egypt and all of Jacob's sons bore their father's body with due sorrow and ceremony to its final resting place.

When they returned to Egypt, the brothers met in council. It was a time that Benjamin had dreaded. He knew that the brothers would not be able to agree on the new leader of the tribe. Feeling ran so high that there was bound to be bloodshed.

As soon as the brothers had gathered, before a word could be spoken that would call forth an angry answer, Benjamin rose and spoke.

"My brothers," he said, "I am the youngest and

should speak last. Forgive my presumption in speaking first. Our tribe is very numerous, God be praised, and is increasing daily. It is really too large for one man to be able to lead successfully. I propose that the tribe be split into twelve parts and that each son of Jacob be head of his own tribe. Thus, the children of Israel will be a confederation of twelve tribes. God himself promised our fathers that we would be a great nation of many tribes. I think the time has come to carry out God's command."

Now, none of Jacob's sons had actually wanted to fight against his brothers. Here was a compromise that could be accepted with honor and without bloodshed. After some discussion, the division of the tribe was agreed upon and each brother went his way in peace.

"Benjamin," Joseph smiled at him, "You're cleverer than I am."

"Oh, no!" said Benjamin, genuinely shocked.

"Oh, yes," said Joseph, "I saw what was coming as well as you did, but I couldn't think of a way to prevent it. You did. Keep thinking, dear brother, Our people will need your brains in the years to come."

The years passed and the children of Israel stayed in Egypt. Living was good and they were protected from enemies. Their numbers increased greatly.One by one, Jacob's sons died. Reuben, Simon, Levi and Judah. Issacher, Zebulon, Dan and Naphtali, Gad and Asher and — finally — Joseph.

Their tribes kept their names but, of all Jacob's sons, only Benjamin was still alive. He was a very old man now, but he found it hard to play the part of the revered ancient sage.

A revered ancient sage should sit and stroke his beard and meditate. Benjamin could generally be found telling stories to a group of children or playing with new born lambs in the pasture. He had no dignity, but people loved him. Old and young had to smile back at him. They couldn't help themselves.

The Pharaoh died and a new Pharaoh ascended to the throne. It was a bad day for the children of Israel. The new Pharaoh cared nothing for the fact that Joseph had served Egypt well, that he had saved the country from famine by his foresight and had greatly increased the Pharaoh's treasury by his cleverness.

The new Pharaoh saw only a large foreign nation living on Egyptian soil. They did not worship Egypt's gods and they were sheepherders, a profession that was looked down upon by Egyptians. These foreigners were exempt from taxes and military service. The Pharaoh felt that they were a potential threat to the Egyptian throne.

Little by little, the Pharaoh began taking away their privileges. He kept increasing their taxes and, more and more, demanded forced labor from the tribesmen of Israel.

A people that has known freedom does not willingly submit to slavery. The indignation of the Israelites flared up time and again. They chased away the grasping tax collectors and fought the slave herders who came to them with whips in their hands.

Benjamin was as horrified by what was happening as by his kinsmen's reaction to events. Everywhere, he heard young people saying, "Why does the Paraoh treat us like this? We were born here. We're Egyptians. We're as good as any of the Pharaoh's other subjects!"

Benjamin knew what he had to do before he died. Of course, he counselled against hot-headed, disorganized resistance to the Pharaoh. The Egyptian army was the greatest and the best in the world at that time. If the Pharaoh willed it, the children of Israel could be wiped out in short order.

Even more, though, Benjamin was horrified by the fact that the young people of the tribes considered themselves Egyptians. Losing their God and their tradition was worse than losing life itself, Benjamin felt.

Young people had always loved listening to Benjamin's stories. Now, he began to organize study circles. Over and over and over again, he told of the God of Abraham, Isaac and Jacob.

Over and over and over again, he repeated the tradition — with every art of the story teller that he knew — that the land of Canaan was their home. They must believe that and teach it to their children and their children's children, if need be.

They must never forget. Some day, their God would lead them out of slavery in the land of Egypt back to freedom in the land of Canaan, their rightful home.

And you know — he was right!

T H E   E N D